For Angel Luis,
Lil' Lil, and Ivy.

The little worm was going

outside to play

...but he had no idea

the hungry bird was out that day!

Heave Ho!

another worm came to help.

The bird cried and cried for help,

...and someone heard!

Now they were twice as strong

the cat

and the bird.

Heave Ho!

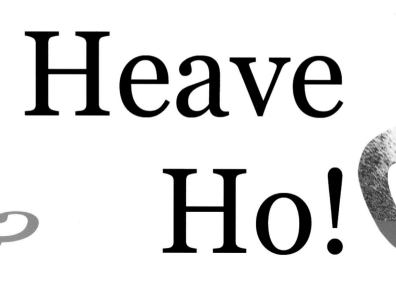

another worm came to help.

Then a dog joined in

Strong
and small.

Heave Ho!

Oh No!

The worms could not move them at all.

But the next worm had an idea!

The dog was mad at the cat.
The cat was mad at the bird.

The bird was so scared
he forgot all about the worm.

They all ran off...

in a hurry

and the worms were free to play.

The End